HA
hee
heee
HA HA
HA HA
HAR
HAR

I brake for banana peels
ZONDERkidz
ZONDERVAN.com/
AUTHORTRACKER
follow your favorite authors

The Silly Family
Written by Katherine Pebley O'Neal
Illustrated by
Laura Huliska-Beith

A happy heart makes the face cheerful.
— Proverbs 15:13

The Silly Family

Requests for information should be addressed to:
Zonderkidz, Grand Rapids, Michigan 49530

Library of Congress Cataloging-in-Publication Data

O'Neal, Katherine Pebley.
The Silly family / written by Katherine Pebley O'Neal ; illustrated by Laura Huliska-Beith.
p. cm.
Summary: The Silly family loves to have a good time, but when they help out with the church picnic and accidentally throw away Mrs. Albright's silly centerpiece, they come to the rescue with their usual good humor.
ISBN-13: 978-0-310-70987-9 (printed hardcover)
ISBN-10: 0-310-70987-3 (printed hardcover)
[1. Jokes–Fiction. 2. Christian life–Fiction.] I. Huliska-Beith, Laura, 1964- , ill. II. Title.
PZ7.O548938Sil 2008
[E]–dc22
2006020709

Art direction & Design: Merit Alderink
Editor: Amy DeVries

Printed in China

08 09 10 11 • 6 5 4 3 2 1

To Corey, Connor, Evan, and Lainey,
who are always too silly.

-K.P.O.

For Mom and Dad:
Thank you for all the love and patience
you gave your loud and messy children!

-L.H.B.

Hee Hee Hee
HA
HA
HA
HA

HA

HA

"Knock, knock!" said Billy.
"Who's there?" asked Lilly.
"Dwayne" said Billy.
"Dwayne, who?" asked Lilly.
"Dwayne the tub, I'm dwowning!" Billy answered.

Mr. and Mrs. Silly laughed so hard they had to hold each other up. Billy, Lilly, and Milly were practically rolling on the floor.

"Excuse me," said a small voice. "Are you here to help with the church picnic?"

"Y-yes, we are," said Mrs. Silly between giggles.

"Oh, good. I'm Mrs. Albright, and I'm in charge of the decorations," she said.

HA

BZZZtt

"It's nice to meet you," said Mr. Silly. He held out his hand.

Bzzzzz! A hand buzzer in Mr. Silly's palm surprised Mrs. Albright.

Mrs. Silly laughed until there were tears in her eyes. Billy, Lilly, and Milly laughed until their sides hurt. Mrs. Albright chuckled uncertainly.

"How can we help you, Mrs. Albright?" Mr. Silly asked.

"Well ..." Mrs. Albright wasn't sure if these silly people could really be helpful. "We have to put tablecloths on all the tables, hang streamers from the trees, tie bows on the chairs, and then place the centerpiece."

"We'll start with the tables," said Mr. Silly. "Come on, kids!"

They got right to work.
"Knock, knock!" said Billy.
"Who's there?" said Milly.
"Interrupting cow," said Billy.
"Interrupting cow, wh—"
"mooo!" interrupted Billy.

The Silly family burst into laughter yet again.
Some of the other church members chuckled quietly.

The Silly family set the tables, put up bows, and threw out an old basket of weeds.

They had to take a short break whenever someone complimented Mrs. Silly's lovely corsage, since they couldn't stop laughing when it squirted water.

And when Mr. Silly slipped on a banana peel, the whole family collapsed in laughter again.

After much hard work, the picnic was ready.

Mrs. Albright felt a tap on her right shoulder. She turned to look, but no one was there.

"Over here," chuckled Mr. Silly, on her left. "Just wondering what else needs to be done."

"Well," said Mrs. Albright. "The congregation should be arriving in fifteen minutes. All we need to do now is put the centerpiece on the main table. Now where is the basket of dried flowers?"

Mr. and Mrs. Silly looked uncomfortable.

The basket of dried flowers sounded familiar.

"Was it sitting on one of the tables while we were decorating?" Mrs. Silly asked.

"Yes!" said Mrs. Albright.

"Could someone have mistaken it for a basket of dead weeds?" asked Mr. Silly.

"Well, I would hope not ..."

Mr. and Mrs. Silly looked from Billy to Lilly to Milly. They all realized they had thrown away the centerpiece.

Mr. Silly went to retrieve it from the trash,

but it was covered with garbage, and it was smashed on the sides.
He slunk back to give Mrs. Albright the bad news.

"You threw away the centerpiece?" wailed Mrs. Albright. "How could you?"

The members of the Silly family looked down at their feet. This wasn't funny.

"Please don't be sad, Mrs. Albright," Lilly said.

"Everything will work out," added Milly.

Suddenly, Billy had an idea. "Mom, what about your corsage?" he asked.

"That's a wonderful idea," said Mrs. Albright. "Mrs. Silly, would you be willing to—"

"Of course," said Mrs. Silly. She unpinned her corsage and placed it in the middle of the head table.

It was perfect.

The picnic was a big success. Everyone liked the pretty decorations. Even the pastor noticed the lovely centerpiece. He leaned forward to smell the flowers.

"Nooooo!" warned Billy. It was too late.

Squirt! Everyone went quiet. Mr. and Mrs. Silly looked from Billy to Lilly to Milly. All eyes were wide.

Then the pastor grinned.

He began to chuckle.

He giggled and snorted.

He hee-hawed and whooped!

The whole congregation erupted into laughter. Some laughed so hard that milk came out their noses. And, of course, the Silly family laughed hardest of all.

Finally, the pastor wiped his eyes and looked around at the congregation. "Well, that proves it," he said. "A joyful heart makes a cheerful face."

Bahaha!
Whee hee hee!
HAR
HAR
HA
HA
SNORt
HoHoHo
Pfthwit!
HeeHee!

The congregation chuckled and giggled their way through the rest of the meal together.

Billy looked up at Mrs. Albright.

"Knock, knock," he said softly.

"Who's there?" asked Mrs. Albright.

"Atch," said Billy.

"Atch who?" asked Mrs. Albright.

"What a sneeze!" answered Billy. "Bless you!"

Mrs. Albright cracked up along with the Silly family. "Bless you too, Billy," she said. "God bless us all."

chitter
chatter
chitter
chatter
HO
HO